PADDINGTON™

THE MOVIE STORYBOOK

3 5 7 9 10 8 6 4

ISBN: 978-0-00-759274-6

First published in Great Britain by HarperCollins Children's Books in 2014

Text by Stella Gurney
Design by Anna Lubecka

All non-film images used under licence from Shutterstock

Based on the Paddington novels written and created by Michael Bond
PADDINGTON™ and PADDINGTON BEAR™ © Paddington and Company Limited / STUDIOCANAL S.A. 2014

Printed and bound in Europe

PADDINGTON™

THE MOVIE STORYBOOK

HarperCollins *Children's Books*

Mr and Mrs Brown and their two children, Jonathan and Judy, are getting off the train at Paddington station after a day out, when Mrs Brown spots a small bear. He's sitting forlornly beneath the Lost and Found sign.

"I'm looking for a home," the bear tells them. He explains that he stowed away on a ship from Peru, and has survived on nothing but marmalade.

"Why don't we find you some help?" asks Mrs Brown kindly.

"Oh yes please!" the bear nods. "That is, if it's no trouble?"

Mr Brown isn't so sure, but he doesn't say anything.

While Mrs Brown and the children go to find help, Mr Brown takes the bear to the station café. He isn't so sure that looking after a bear is a good idea. Henry Brown is a cautious man, and to him this has the makings of a risky situation...

But Mrs Brown can't find anyone to help. "Everyone's gone for the night," she whispers to Mr Brown. "He's going to have to come home with us."

The Browns can't understand the young bear's real name, so they give him an English name: Paddington! Together, they all get into a taxi and head home.

Meanwhile, in London's famous Natural History Museum, a customs official from the docks is making a special delivery to a woman who is very... *fond* of animals.

Stuffed animals, that is. Millicent collects specimens for the museum, and is always on the look-out for something new for her collection. So when the official mentions that he spotted a creature at the docks who seems to have come from Peru and eats marmalade, she's extremely interested.

"I followed him as far as Paddington station," says the customs official, "But then he disappeared. Is he endangered?"

"He is now," answers Millicent ominously.

The taxi drops Paddington and the Browns at their house in Windsor Gardens. There, Paddington meets their neighbour, Mr Curry, who doesn't seem awfully keen on the idea of a bear living next door.

Paddington also meets Mrs Bird, an elderly Scottish relative who lives with the Browns. Her husband used to be in the navy so she likes everything ship-shape.

After the family have shown Paddington around, Mrs Brown asks him why he's all alone and looking for a home.

Paddington explains that his treehouse in Darkest Peru was destroyed by an earthquake that also killed his Uncle Pastuzo. His Aunt Lucy sent him to England to find a new home. He's also looking for an explorer she had befriended many years ago, who had once told her she would always find a warm welcome in London.

Paddington says that the hat he is wearing used to belong to the explorer.

Meanwhile, Millicent is determined to track down the creature seen by the customs official. She manages to break into the security centre at Paddington station...

...puts the guards to sleep with her tranquiliser dart gun....

...and scours the CCTV footage until she spots an animal from Peru who likes marmalade, climbing into a taxi.

"Gotcha!" she says.

Back at Windsor Gardens, Mrs Brown is trying to work out how to track down Paddington's explorer. She thinks perhaps her friend, Mr Gruber, may know about him, so they decide to pay Mr Gruber a visit the following morning.

That night, in his attic bedroom, Paddington gazes out of the window at London. He begins a letter to his Aunt Lucy. "London is not how we imagined it," he writes. "You can't just turn up at the station and find a home. Luckily, I met the Browns, who are letting me stay the night."

The next day, Paddington goes to Mr Gruber's wonderful antiques shop which is full of strange and marvellous things, including a model railway that delivers delicious cocoa and buns!

Mr Gruber hasn't heard of Paddington's explorer – but he does recognise his hat.

"This is no ordinary hat," explains the kind old man. "It was made for a member of the Geographers' Guild."

"What's that?" asks Paddington.

"It is a very famous old explorers' society… they should be able to tell you who it belonged to."

As Mrs Brown and Mr Gruber carry on talking, Paddington notices a man leaving the shop and dropping a wallet.

Chasing after him to return his wallet, Paddington stumbles on to a skateboard, which whisks him through a fancy dress stall on the nearby market. He emerges at top speed, with a dress-up policeman's helmet on, heading fast towards a double decker bus!

Trying to grab on to the pole on the bus, Paddington instead catches hold of a retractable dog lead and an umbrella belonging to one of the passengers. The bus pulls away, with Paddington skateboard-skiing behind!

Suddenly the umbrella opens and Paddington is whisked high into the air.

Luckily, he lands safely on top of the man he was chasing. But the wallet doesn't belong to the man after all. It turns out he is a well-known pickpocket. Soon, the real police step in, and Paddington gets a standing ovation from the crowd!

Back at the Browns' that night, Jonathan and Judy decide to help Paddington find something to wear since – as Jonathan tells him – 'you are technically naked.' They find him the perfect outfit – a blue duffel coat!

Everyone in the family has grown fond of the young bear – even Mr Brown, who promises to take Paddington to the Geographers' Guild the following day to help find his explorer.

Meanwhile, Millicent has been hot on the small bear's trail. She's managed to track down the taxi driver who picked up Paddington and the Browns from Paddington station, and asks him where they live.

"'Fraid I can't tell you that," says the cab driver. "Against the Cabbies' Code, innit."

But when Millicent hangs him upside-down from Waterloo Bridge, he decides the Cabbies' Code isn't so important after all.

Armed with the Browns' address,
Millicent heads straight over to
their house. Determined to capture
Paddington, she spies on him from
a telephone box – until she is
interrupted by nosy Mr Curry.

Millicent explains to him that she's worried
the neighbourhood will become overrun
with bears. With Mr Curry's help, she can make sure the bear is sent back to
where it came from. Mr Curry is delighted to help.

"You could easily keep an eye on the bear, couldn't you?" asks Millicent sweetly.
"Of course," says Mr Curry.
"Then as soon as he's alone, we'll pounce. Partners?"
Mr Curry nods. "Partners."

At the Geographers' Guild, Mr Brown explains that the explorer they're looking for went on an expedition to Darkest Peru. The receptionist says she can't help them.

But Paddington is sure that she is hiding something, and manages to persuade Mr Brown to get back into the Guild, disguised as a cleaning lady!

Once inside the building, they find a reel of film in the Peru section labelled 'Top Secret'. Examining it, Mr Brown recognises the explorer from his hat.

Grabbing the reel, they quickly make their escape.

Later, in Mr Gruber's shop, the Brown family settle down to watch the Geographers' Guild's Top Secret film reel.

It is an old black and white documentary made by the explorer about his visit to Peru, and how he discovered some civilised bears (Aunt Lucy and Uncle Pastuzo, of course!) The explorer's name is Montgomery Clyde.

"Goodbye, my friends," Montgomery calls at the end, tossing his hat to the bears. "If you ever make it to London, you can be sure of a very warm welcome!"

Everyone is excited to see that Paddington's explorer really exists! Now the Browns know the explorer's name, they are even more determined to help Paddington find him. While Paddington starts looking for Montgomery Clyde in the London telephone directories, the family head out to see what else they can find out...

...leaving Paddington at home by himself.

Seeing the Browns leave, Mr Curry calls Millicent immediately.

"The Furry Menace is home alone," he says. "I repeat, the Furry Menace is home alone."

"I'm on my way," she replies.

Millicent wastes no time in getting to
Mr Curry's and she climbs up on to his
roof to get in to next door.
"Just one thing," Mr Curry stammers,
before Millicent kicks the attic hatch
shut. "This *is* all...humane, isn't it?"

"Of course, Mr Curry,"
smiles Millicent,
insincerely, as she
unbuttons her long coat.

Crossing over to the Browns' rooftop, Millicent lowers herself through the skylight...

...but all does not go entirely according to plan. In her haste, she drops her smoke grenade and has to put on a gas mask to protect herself. Just then, Paddington spots her and, thinking she's some sort of monstrous elephant, he lets out a scream and runs into the kitchen.

As he's looking for somewhere to hide, Paddington accidentally knocks against the gas knob on the oven, turning it on.

Kaboom!

Millicent follows him, but can't find the young bear anywhere. As she's searching, the ignition sparks and blows up the escaping gas. Millicent flees the scene.

When the Browns
get home, they find
a fire engine outside.
Paddington tells them
something about an
elephant setting the
house alight. They *want*
to believe him, but it
seems very far-fetched.

That night, Mr Brown lays down the law. "He's putting the children in danger,"
he says. "How can he possibly stay here any longer if we can't even trust him?"

From upstairs, Paddington overhears the conversation. He doesn't want to be any trouble, so sadly he gathers up his suitcase and a list of 'M. Clydes' he has made from the phone book, writes a goodbye note, and leaves the house.

The next morning, Mrs Brown finds Paddington's note.

"It's better this way," says Mr Brown. "He didn't really belong here."

"How can you say that?" demands Jonathan.

"I need to know he's OK," says Mary, heading for the front door.

She goes straight to the police station.
"He's got a red hat on and a blue duffel coat," she says to the desk sergeant. "And he's a bear."

"It's not much to go on," the sergeant replies, doubtfully.

Elsewhere, Paddington's search for the explorer, Montgomery Clyde, seems endless. None of the 'M.Clydes' in the telephone directory turn out to be the right person. He meets Marjorie Clyde ... Morgan Clyde ... then, at last, a result!

"The explorer Montgomery Clyde?" says a woman over the entryphone. "That's my father. Come on in."

The little bear is scarcely able to believe it.

Montgomery Clyde's daughter turns out to be a beautiful, kind lady called Millicent.

She breaks the news to poor Paddington that her father passed away. Paddington is terribly disappointed.

"I suppose I hoped he might give me a home," he confides.

"Oh but *I* can do that," croons Millicent. "You belong somewhere very special. And I know just the place."

"Come along," beckons Millicent. "We're going for a lovely ride."

Paddington climbs into her van and she slides the door shut.

Just then, Mr Curry hurries up with a bunch of flowers for Millicent. He sees Paddington in the van and asks her where they're going.

"I'm sending him where he belongs," replies Millicent impatiently. "Which is the Natural History Museum. Now take your rotten flowers and go!"

Shortly after, the Browns are glumly sitting around their kitchen table when the telephone rings. Mr Brown answers it.

'Hello? This is an anonymous call," says a voice at the other end.
"Oh hello, Mr Curry," replies Mr Brown. Then his expression quickly changes.
"Mr Curry says Paddington's been kidnapped!"
The family all leap to their feet and hurry out to the car.

Meanwhile, Millicent has taken Paddington to the Natural History Museum.

"Welcome to your new home, bear," she announces. "This is a cathedral of knowledge. Every major explorer has added to its glory. But not my father, because he refused to bring back a specimen of your oh-so-precious species."

Millicent goes on to reveal that, because her father came back from his expedition to Darkest Peru without a bear to be stuffed and made into an exhibit, he was thrown out of the Geographers' Guild.
"He could have been rich and famous!" she spits. "But he threw it all away and got a job in a petting zoo!"

"Finally, I realised my father was wrong," continues Millicent. "Every day as I smelled the dung from the donkey pen, I swore I would finish the job my father never did. And now, at last, that day has come! That's right, bear. I'm going to STUFF you!"

Paddington turns and runs...

...but Millicent soon catches him.

Just then, the Browns and Mrs Bird arrive breathlessly at the museum.
Mrs Bird manages to distract the guards while the others break in. Once
inside, Jonathan switches off the lights at the fusebox beneath the building,
throwing the whole museum into darkness.

Puzzled, Millicent goes to investigate, leaving Paddington locked in her stuffing room.

To reach him, Mr Brown decides to climb along a thin ledge outside to try to get in through the window.

"Henry you are NOT going to go out there," pleads Mary.
"Someone's got to," Mr Brown replies grimly. "And that someone is me."
"Do it, Dad!" cheers Jonathan.
After embracing his wife, Henry opens the window and steps out on to the icy ledge…

He looks down.

"Actually, this is insane," he mutters.

He is about to climb back in when he sees his family's faces peering over proudly at him. He has to keep going. Steeling his nerves, he inches his way along the ledge and makes it, despite a couple of hairy moments.

Finally, Mr Brown sees Paddington through the window. "Paddington!" he cries.
"Is that you, God?" asks Paddington, blearily. "It's just, you sound a lot more like Mr Brown than I imagined."

"It *is* Mr Brown!" says Mr Brown.

Eventually, Mr Brown and Paddington manage to escape the stuffing room – but as they're running to join the others, Millicent spots them and shoots at Paddington. He races away, and locks himself in a cleaning cupboard, but Millicent chases after him. "Give up, bear," she calls through the door. There's no way out."

Looking around, Paddington realises that there *is* a way out. He spots two mini vacuum cleaners and, switching them on, he uses the suction power to make his way up a heating shaft and out on to the roof.

The Browns hear him climbing through the shaft, and run up to the roof to meet him there. But Millicent has had the same idea…

Just then, Mrs Bird appears, opening a hatch on to the roof at a crucial moment and knocking Millicent over. The Browns, Mrs Bird and Paddington make their escape.

As a punishment, Millicent is sentenced to 3 months' hard labour in a petting zoo, shovelling donkey dung. The Browns soon discover that the ordeal has brought them all much closer, and they start to have more fun together.

And as for Paddington?

Well, it would seem that the young bear has finally found
a home – with the Browns, at 32 Windsor Gardens.